D0238185

# TETRAX
## THE SWAMP CROCODILE

*With special thanks to Brandon Robshaw*

For Samuel Robin Beeson

www.seaquestbooks.co.uk

ORCHARD BOOKS
338 Euston Road, London NW1 3BH
*Orchard Books Australia*
Level 17/207 Kent St, Sydney, NSW 2000

A Paperback Original
First published in Great Britain in 2014

Sea Quest is a registered trademark of Beast Quest Limited
Series created by Beast Quest Limited, London

Text © Beast Quest Limited 2014
Cover and inside illustrations by Artful Doodlers,
with special thanks to Bob and Justin © Orchard Books 2014

A CIP catalogue record for this book is available from
the British Library.

ISBN 978 1 40832 853 8

1 3 5 7 9 10 8 6 4 2

Printed and bound by CPI Group (UK) Ltd, Croydon, CR0 4YY

The paper and board used in this paperback are natural recyclable
products made from wood grown in sustainable forests. The
manufacturing processes conform to the environmental regulations of
the country of origin.

Orchard Books is a division of Hachette Children's Books,
an Hachette UK company

www.hachette.co.uk

# TETRAX
## THE SWAMP CROCODILE

## THE PRIDE OF BLACKHEART

### BY ADAM BLADE

ORCHARD

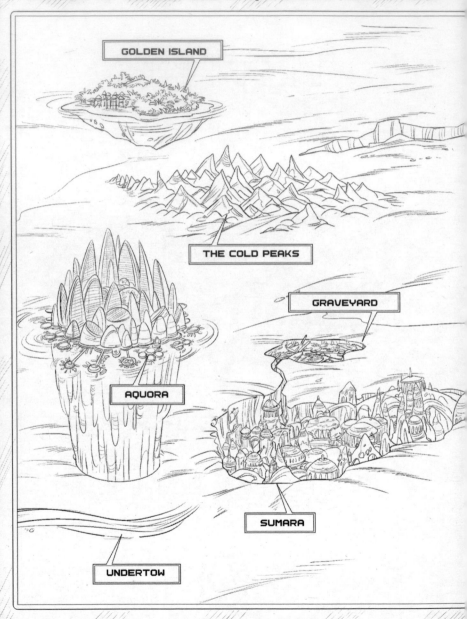

GOLDEN ISLAND

THE COLD PEAKS

GRAVEYARD

AQUORA

SUMARA

UNDERTOW

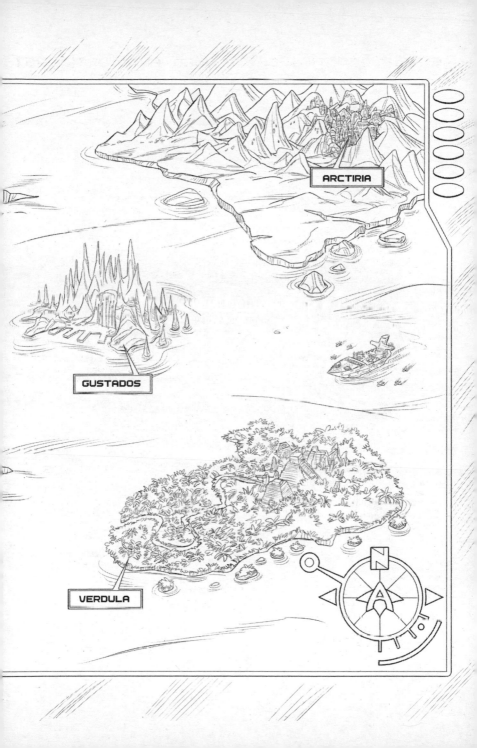

URGENT – PLEASE RESPOND

Mayday! Hostile vessels were detected at 1632 hours off the starboard bow. The *Pride of Delta* has now been boarded by pirates. I am not sure how long we have...

Be aware, the Kraken's Eye will soon be in the hands of the pirates. Please do whatever is necessary to secure the keys. The pirates must not be allowed to operate the weapon.

Rest assured I will not surrender the ship. We will remain in position until we receive a response, or until the ship is taken by force...

END
Message delivered: 1648 hours – Responses: 0

# CHAPTER ONE

# THE AWAKENING

"Goodbye!" Max said.

"Safe journey!" added Lia.

Ko the Sea Ghost smiled. He was a transparent creature with shining green eyes – but Max thought they looked a little sad today. "Goodbye, friends," he said. "Thank you for my stay in your wonderful city."

Lia smiled. Max knew she loved to hear her city praised. Ko had spent several days with them in Sumara. They'd had fun showing him around the Ocean Above, as he called it.

But now it was time for him to return to his home below in the Cavern of Ghosts.

"We'll see you again some day!" Lia said.

Ko parted a clump of seaweed that grew on the ocean bed, and under it Max saw a dark crack. It looked way too small for Ko to fit through – but the Sea Ghost could squeeze his boneless body into the tiniest of spaces. They watched as he swam headfirst into the crack, making himself as thin as a ribbon. Then he disappeared from view.

"That's that, then," Max said, and for a moment he felt quite empty. *I'm going to miss Ko*, he thought. "What shall we do now?"

"Go back to Sumara and take it easy," Lia said. "It's about time we had a rest. I can't wait to beat you at chantra again."

Chantra was a Sumaran game, a bit like chess, played with pieces of coloured coral. Lia had taught Max to play. He still wasn't as good as her, but he was getting better.

"I nearly won last time!" Max said.

"And nearly is as close as you'll get!" said Lia, grinning.

Max climbed onto his new aquabike. He'd salvaged it from the Graveyard in Sumara, where the Sumarans dumped any pieces of unwanted Breather technology they happened to find. He had fixed it up himself, fitting it with an armoured shield around the rider, extra thrusters to increase the speed, and a new horn. Max touched a button and the horn burst out with the opening of his favourite pop song from back on Aquora.

Lia groaned as she climbed onto the back of her pet swordfish, Spike. She put her hands over her ears as Spike shot away fast.

Laughing, Max twisted the throttle and caught her up. Rivet, his robot dog, swam beside him, propellers whirring to keep up. "What's the matter?" Max said. "Don't you like it?"

"It's horrible!" Lia said.

"But that was *Live Forever* by the *Psychotic Sharks*!"

"Never heard of them," Lia said. "And I don't want to! You Breathers don't know anything about music."

"Oh, don't we?" Max said. He sounded the horn again and Lia swerved away from him. Max followed, still laughing.

"Don't make that noise again!" Lia said. "If all your Breather technology is good for is making a horrible racket like that—"

"Technology's good for all sorts of things!" Max said. He slowed down and pulled a headset from his pocket. It had earphones and a mouthpiece. He'd been working on it while Ko was staying with them. "How about this?"

"What's that? Some sort of silly hat?"

Max sighed. "This is a long-distance underwater communicator," he explained. "I fitted a chip in Rivet's head so he can pick up the signal. Watch!"

Rivet was playing with a shoal of silvery fish, well out of earshot. Max slipped the

headset on and spoke into the mouthpiece.
"Hey, Rivet!"

Rivet immediately spun round to face
Max. "Yes, Max?"

"Find me a piece of coral, Riv, and bring
it here."

"Yes, Max! Coming, Max!" Rivet snuffled
around on the seabed, then swam towards
Max, propellers churning. He dropped a
piece of orange coral into Max's lap.

"See?" Max asked Lia. "What do you think
of that?"

"Very clever," Lia said, sounding
unimpressed, "but completely pointless."

A shadow fell across them. Max looked
up and was startled to see a huge creature
looming above. It was a giant fish, round
and brightly coloured. Its pale eyes stared.
Curved spines stuck out from it at all angles,
and it opened its mouth to reveal two rows

of razor-sharp teeth...

Rivet gave an electronic bark. "Bad fish!"

Max hit the brakes. He felt suddenly grateful for his aquabike's armoured shield. Rivet growled at the creature and paddled towards it.

"Stay back, Rivet!" Max said. "It's big

enough to swallow you whole."

Rivet carried on growling.

"I don't think it's dangerous," Lia said. She and Spike followed Rivet.

"Have you seen one before?" Max asked.

"No, but...it doesn't *feel* dangerous."

The creature watched Lia approach. For a moment Max thought it was backing away from her. Then he realised that it was shrinking. Its spines folded into its sides and disappeared. Soon it was smaller than Spike.

"There, there," Lia said, in a cooing voice. "Poor little fellow." She reached out and stroked the fish's head. Right away it nuzzled up against her. "He's a pufferfin," she said. "Only a little one, less than a year old. He inflated because he was frightened. He's wandered away from his shoal, and now he's lost."

"How do you know all that?" Max asked.

"Well, I—" Lia clapped her hand to her mouth. "I can read his thoughts!" Her eyes shone with excitement. "My Aqua Powers are coming at last!

"What do you mean?" said Max.

"It happens to all Merryn when we reach a certain age. We call it the Awakening. Then as we get older, our powers get stronger."

"Wow, that's amazing!" Max said. "Congratulations!"

Lia was beaming with delight. "I'm going to send him a message," she said. "Watch this."

She stared at the fish, her forehead creased in concentration. Suddenly the pufferfin began to swim round and round in circles.

"It works!" Lia said. "I asked him to do that! And this is just the start. Soon I'll be able to speak to animals all over the ocean."

*Just like my headset,* Max thought. *And*

*she said that was completely pointless!* But he didn't want to spoil Lia's special moment.

Rivet's growling got louder again and he pounced at the pufferfin. The little fish darted away fast, and Rivet began to give chase.

"Rivet!" Max called on the Communicator. "Come back!"

Rivet returned, slowly. "Bad, spiky fish!" he growled.

"You just leave it alone," Max said. "I wonder if putting that chip in has messed with his aggression circuits? I'll need to have a look at that."

Lia wasn't listening. "Look, I'm sorry," she was saying to Spike. "Don't take it to heart." She patted him and turned to Max. "He's offended that I spoke to the pufferfin before him. I always knew he was sensitive. It's such fun to be able to talk to him, though!"

BEEP BEEP BEEP BEEP BEEP!

Max's communicator suddenly went crazy, a voice exploding in his ears. "SAVE US! SAVE US! SAVE US!" it said, in Aquoran, then in Merryn, then in several other languages Max didn't recognise.

"What's that noise?" Lia asked. "What's happening?"

"I don't know," Max said, "but it sounds like someone's in trouble."

# CHAPTER TWO

# THE PRIDE OF BLACKHEART

"It's this way," Max said, turning and pointing. He had fitted the Communicator with a location-finder, so that it hummed softly when he headed in the direction of a call. "We have to see if we can help."

Lia agreed. "Let's go!" she said.

"Come on, Riv!" Max said. The dogbot paddled alongside him, still growling a little. Lia pressed her knees into Spike's sides to spur him on, and they set off.

They were travelling over a level plain, with a pale sandy floor not far below them, dotted with black rocks. Shoals of gold and silver fish darted in and out of the rocks, nibbling at the weeds. A school of dolphins came swimming past them in the other direction. Lia smiled and waved at them.

"Could you read their thoughts?" Max asked.

Lia shook her head. "There were too many of them – and I'm still getting used to these Aqua Powers. I just felt they were friendly."

The seabed began to fall away beneath them and a steep shelf descended to the dark, deep ocean floor. Max and Lia stayed up high, where the water was light. The voice continued in Max's head. "SAVE US! SAVE US! SAVE US!"

"We have to hurry," Max said.

Lia nodded. "Looks like we could be at the start of another Sea Quest!" she said. Max felt a tingle of excitement in his chest. He twisted the throttle, getting maximum power from the aquabike. Lia urged Spike on to keep pace.

After a time Max noticed something. "Is it just me, or is it getting warmer?"

"You're right," Lia said. "We must be getting close to the tropical zones."

Max saw that the fish were getting more and more brightly coloured too – there were shoals of orange and white stripy clownfish, and angelfish in vivid blue and yellow. He saw a fish he'd never seen before, a big predator with a crimson crest on its head. It stared at them and then swam quickly away.

"Scared of your aquabike," Lia said. "It's never seen anything like that before!"

The ocean bed rose up to meet them again,

dotted with coral formations of bright red, pink and orange, with tiny fish darting in and out. The sandy floor was covered with waving weeds.

The signal still pounded in Max's earphones: "SAVE US! SAVE US! SAVE US!"

"We must be close now," Max said. "The signal's really strong. And it's coming from above."

He switched the Communicator off. Ahead, he saw the sea floor rise up to the surface. *Looks like an island*, Max thought. *That could be where the signal's coming from.* He turned to Lia and saw that she was already strapping her Amphibio mask on and powering upwards. He pulled back on the handlebars and followed.

In moments, they broke the surface. Max rubbed water from his eyes. The sky was a bright, clear blue. A tropical island rose up before them, covered by a forest of luxuriant green palms.

"That's got to be the place," Max said.

Just then a large wave rushed towards them, lifting Max and his aquabike up high. Max felt as if he'd been snatched up by a giant hand. He tumbled down the other side of the wave. "What on—?"

"Look!" Lia said.

Max managed to regain his balance as the swell died away. He looked where Lia was pointing and saw a huge dark shape looming towards them, pushing the water aside to create waves.

Max gasped. It was a ship. But not just any ship... He'd never seen one this enormous – even bigger than the gigantic ocean-going ones in the docks at Aquora. It was almost as big as the island itself. It looked ultra-modern and streamlined, but not quite

finished, as if it had been taken from the shipyard before the shipbuilders had added the final touches. It was mostly silver-grey, but Max noticed some parts were unpainted and dull, dark metal showed through. There were some uncompleted structures on deck too, like the steel framework of buildings.

With a shudder, Max saw that black skulls

had been painted along the sides. *Not a friendly look*, he thought. The name of the ship was emblazoned on the side: *Pride of Delta*. But the word 'Delta' had been roughly crossed through and the name 'Blackheart' painted below it.

"What does Blackheart mean?" Max asked.

Lia shrugged. "I don't know, but it sounds

like a Breather name to me."

Rivet started barking furiously. He began to swim towards the giant ship, propellers churning up the sea into white foam.

"You silly dogbot!" Max yelled. "Come back!"

Rivet didn't come back. "Going to fight big boat, Max," he barked. "Scare it off!"

*Must be his aggression circuit playing up again*, Max thought. He gunned his aquabike and took off after Rivet. The water was full of thick weeds that reached right up to the surface. They kept catching in the aquabike's motor, slowing him down. The engine squealed in protest. It was no good. Max eased off the throttle and dismounted. He began to swim towards Rivet, pulling himself through the slimy plants, which grasped at him like tentacles.

Rivet was slowing down too, his propellers

clogged by the seaweed. "Bad boat!" he was barking. "Bad, bad boat!"

Max switched his Communicator on. "Stop!" he shouted into the mouthpiece. "Rivet, disable your aggression circuits!"

He heard Rivet's answering bark through the headphones. "Yes, Max. Disabled."

At once the dogbot began to steer away from the ship. Max breathed a sigh of relief. Rivet could easily have been crushed by that enormous vessel.

Max turned and tried to swim back towards his aquabike. But the slimy weeds grabbed at him and he made little progress.

Suddenly a black shadow fell over Max. He looked up in alarm. The ship was passing close by, blotting out the sun.

"Max!" Rivet barked. "Danger!"

He struggled to swim away. But he was still hampered by the weeds. The wave created by the ship tossed him up and down.

Max felt himself being pulled backwards by a mighty current, towards the ship.

"Look out!" Lia shouted. Her voice sounded tiny and remote to Max. The sound of rushing water filled his ears. The ship had passed and he was being dragged along in its wake.

He heard the thunder of its engines growing louder. He got his head out of the water and saw that he was being pulled, very fast, towards an open black metal pipe that protruded from the back of the ship. Its gaping mouth grew bigger and bigger as he got closer.

Max frantically tried to swim clear. His heart thudded, and the muscles in his arms ached. But the pull was far too strong.

All at once the reeds released him and he went tumbling into the mouth of the tunnel,

bouncing from side to side.

Up ahead, he saw an immense metal fan, blades whirring. Powerless to stop himself, Max was swept towards it. In just a few seconds, he was going to be cut to pieces!

# CHAPTER THREE

# AN OLD ENEMY

Max had only moments in which to
act. The deadly blades rushed closer
and closer. He spotted a tiny space at the
very edge of the fan, and remembered Ko
flattening himself to squeeze into the gap
that led to the Cavern of Ghosts. It seemed
impossible, but what else could he do? Max
forced himself against the wall of the tunnel.
The suction whirled him onwards, and he
scraped his back against the wall. He sucked
in his stomach as far as he could.

The chopping blades were almost upon him.

*Here's hoping I don't get shredded*, he thought. He turned his head sideways and closed his eyes, wishing that he, like his Sea Ghost friend, had no bones.

There was a fierce rush of air. Max felt a sharp pain at his chest. Then he felt himself falling. *Is this the end? Am I—*

Before he could finish the thought, he landed with a clang on a metal floor. He opened his eyes.

His heart was thumping madly. But he seemed to be safe, for the time being. He found himself in an engine room, with turbines all around. An electric generator hummed loudly.

Max looked down at his chest. There was a long slash across the front of his wetsuit. He touched it and his fingers came away

sticky with blood. The wound smarted, but it wasn't deep. He was alive!

He took a deep breath and looked around, hunting for a way out.

Nearby he saw a flight of iron steps that led to an upper deck. He was about to go towards it, but then he paused. Maybe the distress signal had come from this ship... But maybe it hadn't. Or maybe the ship, like him, was coming to help whoever had sent the signal. But he couldn't be sure of that. Those skulls painted on the hull didn't look too friendly. He had better be careful.

Max looked up. The ceiling was made of metal grilles, fitted together. He put one foot on the banister and hoisted himself up. He pushed at one of the grilles and it shifted aside. Through the gap he saw a square tunnel, just big enough for a person to crawl through. *Of course, a ship this size would need a ventilation system*, Max thought. *There must be air ducts running all the way through it, connecting all the decks.*

Max hauled himself up into the air duct

and began to crawl along. The metal felt cold on his hands and knees. Soon he came to a shaft going upwards, with metal rungs set into it. He climbed up, and made his way along another duct. He stopped as he saw figures moving beneath him.

Max peered down through the holes in the grille. The room below looked like the ship's bridge. There was an array of hi-tech control panels, instruments, computer screens and a retro-style ship's wheel. Two men were standing there. One had a long black beard, the other a shaggy moustache. They both wore high-impact armour padding. One had a set of knives strapped to his belt, and the other had a hook for a hand. They were talking, but Max couldn't make out the words. Silently he switched his Communicator on and their voices came through loud and clear.

"Is it time to feed them bilge-rats down in the brig?" said the one with the hook.

"They got fed yesterday, matey. Today they go hungry!" replied the other.

"Dunno why we took prisoners anyway. Now the ship's ours I'd rather rip their gizzards out and feed 'em to the fish!"

"Gotta have some prisoners on a pirate ship," said the one with the black beard. "Tradition, innit?"

*So they're pirates!* Max thought. And not friendly pirates like Max and Lia's old friend Roger, either. It was a good thing Max hadn't run up those stairs and announced himself. He'd have been locked up with the other prisoners.

"Anyway, now we got the ship," the pirate with the hook said, "what are we gonna do with it? We never get told nothing."

"Why don't you ask Cap'n Blackheart,

then?" said the pirate with the beard.

"Maybe I will. I ain't afeard."

"Then you oughta be. Cap'n Blackheart's the foulest devil on the high seas, and a devil that don't like being questioned, neither—"

The automatic door to the bridge swished open. Max saw a tall pirate enter, wearing a long coat and plenty of jangling gold jewellery. One leg was of shining metal from the knee down – a robotic peg leg. The pirate had tangled dark hair, and held a whip with a bunch of thongs like the stingers of a jellyfish. It glittered and sparked as the pirate swished it – an electric cat-o'-nine-tails, Max realised. Another person came in behind the pirate, but from this angle Max could not see who it was. He edged forward to get a better view, moving as silently as he possibly could. If he were discovered he didn't expect a friendly welcome.

The first two pirates immediately snapped to attention.

"Did I just hear someone mention my name?" Captain Blackheart said, in a soft, silky voice – and Max suddenly realised that Captain Blackheart was a woman.

"We...we was just saying what a great Cap'n you was, Cap'n," stammered the pirate with the hat.

"Belay there!" Captain Blackheart said sharply. "Don't try and flatter me, you cowardly swabs!"

She swished her electric cat-o'-nine-tails at the pirates. They jumped back, trembling.

"So what were you really saying?"

The bearded pirate pointed at the one with the hook. "He said he was going to ask you about our plans, now we got this ship—"

Captain Blackheart stepped in close to the pirate with the hook. A crackle of sparks ran through her electric cat-o'-nine-tails and the pirate cringed.

Then Max saw the figure who'd been standing behind the Captain: a tall, broad-shouldered man with a grey beard and

piercing, deep-set dark eyes. Max clapped his hand to his mouth to stop himself from crying out. It was his uncle, the Professor!

"So, you question my strategy?" said Captain Blackheart softly.

"No, I was just—"

The cat-o'-nine-tails flicked out. There was a loud *CRACK* and a spark, and the pirate yelped and clutched his ear.

The Professor cleared his throat. "Perhaps it would be advisable to explain our plans to the crew now, Cora," he said. "We are close to our destination and—"

"Belay there!" Captain Blackheart swung round to face him. "Don't get smart with me, Professor. I'll have you keelhauled if you get on the wrong side of me."

They stared at each other defiantly for a few moments. But it was the Professor who dropped his gaze first.

"All the same," Cora Blackheart said finally, "this time you have a point. Tell them yourself."

"Yes, Captain," the Professor said submissively. "Well, men, it's simple enough. With the weapon on board this ship we're strong enough to take on the Delta Quadrant Alliance – and win! And we start by attacking the weakest Alliance city – Verdula. They're guarding a certain key, and once we have that, well, the other cities will be easy meat."

*So that's the plan!* Max thought. *Maybe Verdula is where the distress signal came from...* They must have seen the dangerous ship approaching. So to save the island he'd somehow have to defeat this ship full of pirates. He began to edge backwards, trying not to think about the rest of the pirates' plan. He'd learned the names of the four Delta Quadrant Alliance cities back at school.

Verdula, Arctiria, Gustados...and Aquora. But right now he needed to get away without being spotted, so that he could link up with Lia again and work out what to—

Suddenly, Max's Communicator crackled into life.

"Max? Where Max? Max alive?" It was Rivet.

Max winced at the noise, switched the Communicator off and shoved it into his back pocket. But it was too late.

The Professor looked up.

Captain Blackheart slashed her whip at the ceiling. The electric thongs hit the panel in front of Max and it clattered to the floor.

Max froze. Four faces stared up at him.

# CHAPTER FOUR

# THE KRAKEN'S EYE

Captain Blackheart swung her cat-o'-nine-tails again. There was a loud *CRACK* and Max felt the panel directly underneath him give way. He crashed to the floor, rolling as he landed, but the impact still knocked all the breath out of him.

"Max!" the Professor said. "How kind of you to drop in!"

Cora turned to the Professor and frowned. "You know this swab?"

"Oh, I know him! He's my favourite nephew – aren't you, Max?"

Max staggered to his feet, too breathless to answer.

"What's he doing here?" Cora demanded.

"Don't ask me," the Professor said. "He has the knack of popping up in the most unexpected places. Knowing him as I do, I'd suggest searching him for hidden weapons."

"Jump to it!" Captain Blackheart barked.

The two pirates approached, grinning. Max thought fast. He mustn't let them find his Communicator. That was his only chance of getting some help from outside.

He clapped his hand to the breast of his wetsuit, where he kept the Pearls of Honour. "You can search all my pockets," he said, "but don't bother with this. It's nothing."

"See what he's got there!" Cora rapped out.

"No, no, you can leave this," Max said. "Just

look in my pockets!"

The pirate with the hook grinned and dragged Max's hand away. With his hook, he seized the Pearls of Honour. "Well, what have we here?" He dropped the Pearls and

stamped on them, smashing them to pieces with his boot.

Max didn't like losing the Pearls of Honour. They had the power to call any sea creature to his aid. But it was worth the sacrifice. Now the pirates had found the Pearls, they thought they'd got everything – but he still had the Communicator, safe in his back pocket.

"You have to be smarter than that to outwit us!" said Hook-Hand. He grabbed hold of Max's hyperblade and ripped it from his belt.

Cora Blackheart turned to the Professor. "What shall we do with your nephew, then?"

"Lock him up in the brig," the Professor said. "We'll decide what to do with him after Verdula."

"Why are you attacking Verdula?" Max demanded. "What have they done to you?"

"They got a special key there," said Hook-Hand, "and once we got that the other cities will be easy meat!"

Captain Blackheart slashed her electric whip at him, coiling it round his neck. He howled in pain as she dragged him down to the floor. "Shut your mouth!" she hissed. "Or *you'll* be easy meat. For the sharks!"

Without warning she spun round and flicked the cat-o'-nine-tails at Max. The flails touched the wound on his chest. Pain shot through it, so severe he almost collapsed.

"And you, don't ask questions!" said Captain Blackheart. "Mess with me, and you'll end up dead. I'm not joking." She turned to Max's uncle. "Get him out of here. Take him to the brig and lock him up."

Max had never seen his uncle obey someone else's orders before. But without a word, he put his hand on Max's shoulder and led him from the bridge.

"So nice to see you again, Max," he said

with an evil smile. "I'd hoped our most recent battle wouldn't be our last. What do you think of the ship? It's state-of-the-art, you know."

Max didn't answer. He was trying to take in his surroundings. The corridor was wide and high, lit by a white plasma ceiling. There were antiques, paintings, statues and jewellery on display everywhere – stolen booty, Max guessed.

"So you take orders from the Captain now?" he asked. Maybe he could anger the Professor into giving up more information...

"I don't take orders!" snapped the Professor. "Cora is useful, that's all."

"Yeah? She sounded like the boss to me," Max said. "Are you sure it's you using her, not the other way round?"

"The pirates are going to make me rich and powerful," said his uncle.

"I'll believe that when I see it," Max said.

"Oh, is that so?" the Professor said angrily. "Let me show you something!"

He steered Max down a side corridor, pushing him on ahead. Max noticed a door to his right marked POD CHAMBER. *Escape pods*, he thought. *Might be useful.*

They came to a black iron door. The Professor opened it with a keycard hanging from his belt, and it slid aside to reveal a flight of stairs. "Up. You first."

At the top was another door. The Professor opened this with his keycard too. "Now tell me what you see, Max."

They were in a cavernous hall, with a huge black metal tube running down the centre. At one end it was anchored on a metal platform covered in consoles, wires and flickering screens. The other end pointed out of a massive porthole. It looked like the barrel of

a cannon, Max realised suddenly – but surely no cannon could be that big?

"Lost for words?" the Professor said. "This is the Kraken's Eye. It can destroy a whole city with one blast. But these ignorant pirates can't operate it without me."

Max suddenly realised something. "You can't operate it either," he said.

The Professor glared at him. "What do you mean?"

"You stole this ship, didn't you? From the Delta Quadrant Alliance." There was nowhere else the pirates could have got this ship from. "You've stolen it and now you can't make it work! That key the pirate said you were going to get from Verdula...you need it for something. It's for this, isn't it?"

"Smart boy," the Professor said, grudgingly. "Yes, the Kraken's Eye needs a key to activate it. Each of the four cities of the Delta Quadrant Alliance holds one. But that's no problem. Once we get a key, Cora and her pirates will rule the Delta Quadrant. And everything below the waves will belong to me! The Merryn will all be my slaves."

"You really think that any of the cities will just hand over their key?" asked Max.

"They're fools if they don't."

"Whatever you say," said Max, with a sarcastic smile. "I don't think you know how to get that key. You're all talk."

His uncle's lips set in an angry line. "Follow me. I'll show you something to wipe that grin off your face!"

He led Max to an elevator and the doors swished open. The Professor motioned Max inside and in silence they descended what felt like several decks. At last there was a ping and the doors opened again.

"Have a look around, Max," his uncle said. "And then admit that I'm a genius."

They were in a big, dimly lit room. One whole wall was made of toughened glass, and through it Max saw the dark ocean. The room itself was filled with glass tanks, each one full of greenish liquid. Max gasped in horror when he saw the strange creatures floating in the tanks. There was a squid-like creature with countless tentacles. Something else looked like a shark with three mouths, each with twenty rows of teeth. There was a jellyfish with a barracuda's head.

"I created them, Max," his uncle said, "using robotics and genetic engineering. They are my new Robobeasts. When they're fully grown they'll be the most powerful I've

ever created, and they'll attack any island
city I ask them to."

Max felt sick. He imagined what Lia
would say if she could see this. The horrible
disregard for nature would make her furious.

"I can see you're impressed," the Professor

said. "But you don't know the best bit. My first creation, Tetrax, is already fully grown! And I sent it out to attack Verdula, just before you arrived!"

Before Max could answer, an ear-splitting alarm went off.

BEEP! BEEP! BEEP! BEEP!

Cora Blackheart's voice came crackling over the ship's address system.

"Action stations! The ship is under attack! Hostile approach on starboard bow!"

The lab doors opened and a gang of pirates rushed in. "Professor! We got to repel an attack!"

The Professor's mouth opened in surprise. "What?"

One of the pirates pointed at the glass wall. "Look!"

Max turned and saw a strange dark shape coiling through the water towards them.

# CHAPTER FIVE

# ATTACK OF THE GIANT OCTOPUS

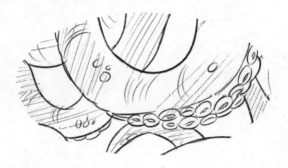

*An octopus!* That's what it was. The creature was bright red, with massive, suckered tentacles reaching out towards the ship.

Max's heart leaped with relief as he spotted Lia on Spike, tiny next to the octopus. Rivet was bobbing beside them, metal tail wagging. Lia caught sight of Max and grinned, giving a thumbs-up sign. *Of course!* Max thought. *She's using her new Aqua Powers to get the octopus to attack the ship!*

The next second there was an almighty *THUD* as the octopus cannoned against the hull of the Pride of Blackheart. Max felt the floor slide from under his feet, and he crouched down low. The pirates stumbled and fell over one another, and the Professor had to clutch at the side of one of the glass tanks to stay upright.

The giant octopus wasn't nearly as large as the ship – but it was still big and strong, and heavy enough to make an impact. It backed off and readied itself for another attack.

Cora's voice came over the address system again. "Professor – deal with this situation immediately! Immediately, do you hear?"

The octopus crashed into the ship again. The pirates who had just got up fell back down. Hook-Hand swore loudly. The Professor sagged against the side of the tank as the floor rocked beneath him.

It was now or never. Max darted forward and plucked the keycard from his uncle's belt.

"No!" shouted the Professor. He made a grab at Max, but Max ducked under his outstretched arm and ran for the door.

"Get him!" shouted the Professor.

The pirates lunged after Max, but he made it to the door just ahead of them and opened it with a swipe of the keycard.

Half a second later the door slid shut in his pursuers' faces – but he had only got a short way down the corridor when he heard it opening again, and pirates' footsteps thudding behind him.

"We got him, lads!" shouted Hook-Hand.

Max thought fast. The corridor was lined with more of the pirates' booty, so as he ran, Max pulled things down behind him. He toppled a statue of a gigantic seahorse, a painting of a moon, some musical instruments and a gilded shark's skeleton.

There were crashes, clatters and clangs as the pirates collided with the stolen goods and fell over. Max heard them shouting and swearing as he turned a corner and ran up a flight of steps, his heart racing.

At the top, a pirate suddenly appeared in front of Max. He was a giant of a man with a white beard and most of his teeth missing. He drew a blaster from his belt and pointed it at Max. "Going somewhere, sonny?"

There was another thud and the ship rocked again. The pirate tottered. Quickly, Max grabbed the handrail and clung on as the pirate plunged down the stairs past him.

Max reached a junction and looked about him. *Left or right?* He had a feeling that the Pod Chamber was to the right. He set off at a run, and then he saw it, down a side passage.

He opened the door with the keycard and raced in to find a large room with a row of twenty white, streamlined escape pods, like miniature subs. Each pod was on its own chute which led down to a central steel portal. It had to lead out to the open sea.

*Phew!* Max thought. *Made it!*

He jumped into one of the pods. His guess was that if he could start it, the pod would slide down the chute and the portal would open automatically. He pressed the ENGAGE button.

Nothing happened.

There was the sound of running steps, then a furious banging at the door.

"Open up! We know ye're in there!"

Max bent over the dashboard of the pod, heart pounding. He switched on the monitor and the screen glowed green. There had to be a way to get into the system and make the thing work!

The banging got louder. Max glanced over and saw the door shuddering with each blow.

He went into Settings. ACCESS DENIED. He found the menu for Operating Systems, and clicked on Preferences.

*Yes!* MANUAL OVERRIDE!

He pressed the button.

*No!* ENTER PASSWORD.

There must be a way to get round that. But Max wasn't used to this system. It was going to take a while to figure out, and—

The door suddenly gave way and slid open, and a gang of pirates came stomping in. "Now we got you, you scurvy dog!"

Max stood up in the pod, ready to fight. But there were so many of them, and he had nothing to defend himself with.

"I'm going to teach you the true meaning of the word 'pain'!" said Hook-Hand.

Suddenly, Max heard a rending sound behind him. He turned to see the steel portal at the end of the chute burst open. Water rushed in. A great scarlet tentacle came probing in through the gap.

The pirates fell back in terror.

Before Max could move, the tentacle snaked

towards him and wrapped itself around the pod. Max held on tight as the pod went sliding out through the portal and into the rushing, cold black water.

Max gasped. The sea flooded his gills and he breathed salt water once again.

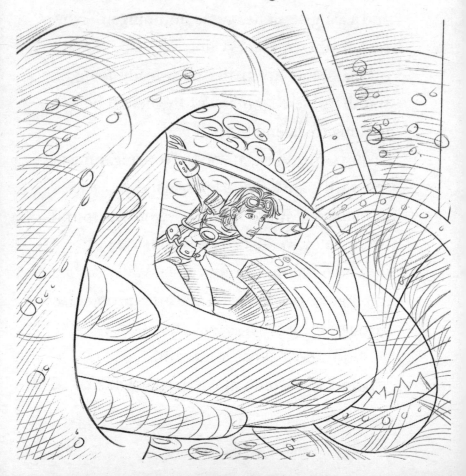

"Max! Max safe!" It was Rivet. He came swimming towards Max, little legs churning and steel tongue hanging out. And then came Lia, sitting astride Spike.

Max pulled himself out of the pod and swam to meet them.

"Thanks, Lia!" Max said. "You saved me. I couldn't start the pod."

"That's the trouble with technology." Lia smiled. "You can't rely on it. But Aqua Powers never let you down!"

"OK, I'll give you that one," Max said. "But listen, we have to hurry. There's a Robobeast on its way to attack Verdula. We've got to try to help the islanders!"

"What sort of Robobeast?" Lia asked.

"I don't know," Max said. He thought of the strange creatures in the tanks in the Professor's laboratory, and shuddered. "But whatever it is, I don't think it's going to be pretty."

# CHAPTER SIX

# JOURNEY INTO THE JUNGLE

Lia stared into the octopus's golden eyes. "Thank you for your help – you are free to go!"

The octopus turned away in a tangle of writhing arms. It waved the tip of one its tentacles at Lia and Max, as if saying goodbye. Then it suddenly squirted out a jet of water and moved away backwards at amazing speed, its tentacles trailing out straight behind it.

"Hey, that's fast!" Max marvelled, and then he remembered his aquabike. "We need to go back to the weeds to get my bike," he told Lia.

"Of course," Lia said. "Follow us. It's quite a way."

"Mind if I hitch a ride, Rivet?"

"Jump on, Max!" barked Rivet.

Max sat astride Rivet's chunky iron body and hunched down low. Rivet's paws began to whir as he doggy-paddled alongside Lia and Spike.

As they travelled, Max told Lia about what had happened on the *Pride of Blackheart*. "And we have to hurry," he finished, "because this Tetrax is on its way to Verdula. It may be there already."

"But what is it?" Lia asked.

"No idea," Max said. "But the Professor said these new Robobeasts are the most powerful he's ever created."

Soon the water became shallower and the weeds thicker. They were approaching the island. Max broke the surface and saw his aquabike sticking up out of a mass of slimy seaweed. Behind it, in the middle distance, he saw the island of Verdula, covered in thick green jungle. He jumped off Rivet and half swam, half waded towards the bike.

Max stripped the weeds away from the aquabike's motor, while Rivet pulled away great strands of seaweed with his iron jaws. Between them they towed the bike back into open water. Max gunned the engine into life and dived beneath the waves to rejoin Lia and Spike.

"Where to?" Lia asked.

Max pulled the Communicator from his pocket and switched it on. The distress signal came in loud and clear: "SAVE US! SAVE US! SAVE US!"

"We have to follow this signal," Max said. He slipped the headset on. "This way."

They skirted around the island. The hum of the location-finder grew louder in Max's ears. At the same time he felt a current of slightly warmer water coming away from the island. *It must be a river, flowing out into the sea.*

"We go upstream," Max said, pointing.

They turned and headed up the river, against the current. The water resisted them, but Spike's strength and the aquabike's engines helped push them onwards. Max saw that poor Rivet was struggling, and pulled him up onto the back of his bike.

Soon the water became murkier. It was getting hard to see anything. Max surfaced, and when he'd rubbed the river water from his eyes he saw that they were travelling through a steamy green jungle. The banks on either

side were thick with trees and creepers, and
Max heard the cries of monkeys and macaws.
A moment later Lia's head popped up to join

him. She was wearing the Amphibio mask.

"It's getting too shallow," she said.

"Then we'll have to wade," Max replied.

Lia slipped off Spike's back. They made their way upstream, with Max pulling the aquabike along beside him. Soon the river only reached to their waists. Rivet and Spike swam with them, Spike's dorsal fin sticking out of the water. The jungle trees hung over head, throwing a green gloom over everything.

Max wondered if Tetrax was somewhere near...and if so, what kind of deadly creature it would be.

The jungle was full of noises: insects squeaking, birds calling, trees rustling. Every sound made Max's skin prickle. He was sure they were being watched. He kept peering through the trees on either side, but couldn't see anything. But that wasn't surprising. The foliage was thick enough to hide a thousand pairs of watching eyes.

The river got shallower. It was only halfway up their thighs. The whole of Spike's back stuck out of the water now. The mud at the bottom got thicker, and the creepers overhanging the river got denser. Max longed for his hyperblade to cut a way through, but there was nothing to do except push and squeeze and dodge their way around.

"*YAARRGII!*"

The scream cut through the silence like a knife. Max and Lia stopped and stared at each other.

"Noise, Max!" Rivet said.

"What was it?" Lia asked. Her eyes looked worried above her Amphibio mask.

"Maybe some kind of animal," Max said. But he had never heard any animal scream like that. It had sounded human. Sort of.

"*YAARRGH!*" The scream came again, and again, and again, and suddenly the jungle was full of screams on all sides.

The next instant, bodies were dropping from the trees, jumping from the banks and splashing into the river, in front of them, behind them, all around. Max had a confused impression of monkey-like figures, with long, sinuous arms, big luminous eyes and tattooed faces. Rivet began to bark furiously. Max tensed, ready to fight.

And then someone jumped on his back.

Max staggered in the water. A moist, sticky arm wrapped itself around his neck. He scrabbled at it and tried to pull it away – but though the person on his back was small, whoever it was had a frightening, wiry strength.

Two more of the strange people had grabbed Lia's arms. Another three had

surrounded Rivet and were pointing sharp
wooden spears at him.

Max struggled to breathe.

"Help!" he spluttered to Lia. "Use...your Aqua Powers...tell him..."

He saw Lia's forehead wrinkle as she concentrated.

The grip on Max's throat just got tighter. He felt a pain in his lungs.

"I can't...breathe... You have to..."

"I'm trying!" Lia said. "He won't listen!"

Max felt as though he was about to black out. He saw Lia's face screwing up as she tried her best to get through to his attacker—

And suddenly the deadly grip loosened.

Max sucked in a huge lungful of air. He coughed. His hand went to his aching throat, rubbing it gently as he recovered his breath.

Max's attacker slipped off his back and stood in front of him. He was lithe and slight, with long limbs like a monkey's, and he only came up to around Max's chin. His face was tattooed in swirly patterns. He wore a loincloth of plaited reeds around his middle, and a necklace of sharks' teeth hung on his bare chest. He glared at Max and spoke in a strange, chattering tongue.

"I understand him now," Lia said. "He's the leader of these people and his name is Naybor. He thinks we're enemies. They've seen the strange giant ship, and seen humans like you on the deck. And they don't like the look of Rivet, either."

"Tell them we're here to help them," Max said. "Say we heard their signal. We're on their side against the pirates. Tell them they have to give us the key to the Kraken's Eye – otherwise the pirates will come and take it from them!"

Lia narrowed her eyes at Naybor. Max almost imagined he could see her invisible thoughts streaming towards him.

Naybor frowned at her. Then he burst into a chattering laugh. All the other jungle people joined in.

"Why's he laughing?" Max demanded.

Lia sighed. "He says we must think they're idiots," she said. 'They're supposed to protect the key, not give it away to the first person who comes along and asks for it!"

Max could see their point. How could he persuade the Verdulan people that they were on their side – that they really were here to help?

Suddenly, there was a massive splash downriver. Spray fell and drenched Max. The Verdulan people screamed and jumped for the bank, pulling themselves up into the trees with their long, sinuous arms. Rivet growled – and even he sounded scared.

"Uh-oh," Lia said.

With a sinking sensation in his gut, Max turned round to see what was behind them.

*Tetrax!*

# CHAPTER SEVEN

# THE SWAMP MONSTER

A gigantic creature was standing up in the river, as tall as the trees around it. It looked like some sort of crocodile, Max thought – but it was bigger than any crocodile could possibly be, and it had six legs. It was standing on two of them, and the other four waved around. Sprouting from its back was a huge wing-like sail, but the creature was far too big to fly. It was a poisonous green colour except for its belly, which was a sickly yellow.

Some kind of metal device, a bit like the muzzle of a cannon, was fixed on the top of its head. It opened its terrifying jaws, and Max saw that its teeth were silver and sharp as sabres. They fizzed and crackled with electricity, the bright sparks lighting up the knife-like fangs.

Max wrinkled his nose. The beast gave off a disgusting smell, a mixture of swamp mud, blood and a sharp, electrical odour.

"It's...horrible," Lia breathed. "Worse than the others."

"I know," Max said. "But we have to take it on. If we don't beat it, there's nothing to stop the pirates getting the key for the Kraken's Eye, and then..."

Max heard the islanders shouting from the trees. A hail of wooden spears and arrows flew at Tetrax from every direction, but they bounced off the Robobeast's armoured hide. Tetrax let out an angry roar. Its great long head swung round to the direction the spears had come from, and with a strange humming sound, a beam of green light shot

out from the metal tube on its head.

As Tetrax's head turned, there was a flurry
in the trees and two of the Verdulan people
were dragged out, caught inside the green
ray. Slowly they were pulled through the air

towards the creature's jaws…

*A tractor beam!* Max thought. *Tetrax uses it to drag people into its mouth!*

The Verdulans kicked and screamed as they were carried helplessly towards Tetrax's hungry jaws. How could Max save them?

He looked around and saw a dead branch lying on the bank nearby. Grabbing it, he ran along the bank and jabbed it up at the monster's head. For an instant, the jagged bit of wood broke the tractor beam and the two Verdulans fell into the river. But at the same time the tractor beam dragged at the branch, tearing it from Max's hands with ease and pulling it into Tetrax's jaws.

The Robobeast snarled and chomped the branch into splinters. Then it strode forward on its powerful hind legs and, dipping its head, snapped at the two Verdulans who were desperately swimming away. They made it

to the bank and swung up into the trees...
but one of them was too slow. Tetrax lunged
forward and grabbed hold of his trailing
arm. The Verdulan screamed. With horror
Max saw Tetrax bite the arm clean off and
swallow it like a strand of spaghetti.

Lia and Max exchanged a glance. "We've
really got a fight on our hands," she said.

"It must have a weak spot somewhere,"
Max said. He tried to sound more confident
than he felt. "If I could get close enough to
see its workings—"

"Good idea!" Lia said. "I'll distract it!"

Before Max could stop her she ran towards
the monster, which was now stalking along
the river, snapping at the trees. It seemed to
have got a taste for Verdulan flesh now.

Max caught up and grabbed Lia by the
shoulder.

"No," he said. "If someone's going to

distract that beast it had better be Rivet. If Tetrax chomps him, at least I can rebuild him!"

"Well...all right," Lia said reluctantly. "But you'd better hurry!"

"Riv?" Max said. "Turn your aggression circuit back on, OK? And then go and get that monster!"

"Yes, Max!" There was a click, and Rivet's eyes flashed red. He started barking ferociously. "Bad croc!"

Tetrax had scrambled up the bank now, and was crashing through the forest in search of more Verdulans to eat. They were running and swinging through the forest to get away, occasionally turning back to hurl spears at the Robobeast.

Rivet ran after Tetrax, barking madly. Max followed as fast as he could. Finally Rivet caught the monster up and clamped his iron jaws on Tetrax's foot.

The Robobeast gave an angry bellow. With one fast movement it shook the dogbot off, sending him flying into the undergrowth. Then it fixed the tractor beam on Rivet and raised him up, dragging the dogbot towards its jaws.

*Oh no!* Max thought.

He swarmed up a nearby creeper, until he was level with Tetrax's head, then stared into the monster's gaping mouth. Sparks flew from its metallic-looking teeth. Even the inside of its mouth seemed to be coated in a silvery substance. The tractor beam tube was fused into the Robobeast's flesh, with no sign of a join.

Rivet was nearly within reach of those jaws. The monster's mouth opened wider. Rivet barked and struggled but could not break free of the beam.

*I sent Rivet into danger*, Max thought. *There's no way I'm going to let him be eaten by that thing!*

He braced his feet against a nearby tree trunk and pushed off as hard as he could. He swung right into Rivet, knocking him clear

of the tractor beam.

The dogbot tumbled down to the forest floor. Max grabbed at a branch as he fell. The branch bent, then snapped, but it was enough to break his fall and he landed safely. There was an agonising pain in his leg. It took him a moment to realise why – the electric current had shot out from Tetrax's teeth and hit him. It was like being scalded.

Tetrax's huge head swung towards him. Max tried to leap to his feet but his leg was numb and he collapsed again. The slavering, crackling jaws were right above him now.

There was a thud as a rock bounced off Tetrax's snout.

"Got you!" Lia shouted.

For an instant the Robobeast turned, and Max rolled away to safety. The monster's jaws snapped shut a hair's breadth from him.

Max crawled into the undergrowth as

Tetrax swung away into the forest, in pursuit of the Verdulans, who were still hurling spears from the shadows of the trees.

"Max! Are you all right?" Lia helped him to his feet.

Rivet came scampering up, unharmed by his fall. "Max? Max hurt?"

"I'll be all right," Max said. "Good shot with that rock, Lia!" He tried to rub the numbness from his leg. "It's got some kind of electric current in its teeth. Good job it didn't chomp you, Rivet, or your circuits would have been totally fried, and—" He stopped.

"What?" said Lia. "What is it?"

"I think I have an idea," said Max.

# CHAPTER EIGHT

# THE JAWS OF DEATH

"Whatever your idea is," Lia said, "we need to work fast!"

As she spoke, Tetrax swept its tractor beam through the jungle again. Two Verdulans were pulled from the trees and dragged up to its mouth. The mighty jaws clamped shut and the screaming stopped.

Max turned away, unable to watch. "The Robobeast has a massive electrical power source," he said. "That's what makes it so strong. But that's also a weakness. Any electrical system can be shut down if you hit it with a big enough electromagnetic pulse!"

"With a what?" Lia said. "An electric maggot's pulse?"

"I'm going to need a power source," Max said. He took off his Communicator. "I guess I'll have to sacrifice this."

"I think it'll be worth it!" Lia said.

Tetrax was thrashing around in the jungle, searching for more islanders to eat. Three Verdulans broke cover to throw spears at it and were pulled, screaming, towards the monster's jaws.

Max set the Communicator on a tree stump and opened it up. He had to work fast – every second's delay meant more deaths. He tried to turn the dial that altered the power settings, but the workings were tiny and without tools it was incredibly fiddly.

"What are you doing?" Lia asked urgently.

"I programmed this with a self-destruct setting," Max said, "in case it fell into the wrong hands. It'll send out a small burst of energy. But if I can jack up the power, it'll stop other electrical stuff working too. Including Tetrax. That is, if I can get him to…well, swallow it."

"I never thought I'd say this," Lia said, "but I think we'll have to give your technology a chance."

Tetrax roared. Its head swung round and a pair of cold reptilian eyes fell on Max as he kneeled there, fiddling with the headset. The Robobeast took one huge stride forward.

"I'll buy you some time!" Lia said. She ran in front of the monster, waving and screaming at it. It cocked its head and stared at her. Then the tractor beam swept towards her.

Lia ducked under it and dived into the river.

Tetrax went down on all six legs and slid in after her.

Max was sweating. His fingers couldn't get a grip on the tiny wheel he needed to turn.

Rivet barked at Tetrax from the bank, but

Tetrax ignored him and lunged at Lia. The Merryn princess just swam clear in time. There was a flurry in the water. Max looked up briefly and saw that Spike was attacking Tetrax, jabbing at the monster's hide with his sharp bill.

They couldn't hope to defeat Tetrax or even hurt it much, but if they could just keep it occupied a little longer...

*There!* Finally, the wheel had turned!

"Rivet!" Max shouted. "Get in the river – I don't want the pulse to affect you!" The dogbot dived into the water.

Max ran along the bank, half stumbling on his numb leg. "Come and get me, Tetrax!" he said. "Let's see what you've got!"

The swamp crocodile ignored him. It thrashed the water with its powerful tail. The impact sent both Spike and Rivet flying out of the river to land with a splash downstream.

Then Tetrax turned its hungry eyes on Lia again.

Max looked around and saw that one of the fleeing Verdulans had dropped a bow and a few arrows on the bank. He picked up the weapon and fitted an arrow, but it was surprisingly hard to pull the string back. His first attempt went wide, disappearing into the river. The second arrow slammed into a tree trunk. Tetrax ignored both.

Desperate, Max flung aside the bow, sending it bouncing off a rock. Suddenly he remembered how Lia had distracted the crocodile earlier. He snatched up the rock and hurled it, hitting Tetrax just above the eye.

That got the Robobeast's attention.

Tetrax snarled and rose to its full height again. It stepped out of the river and its tractor beam picked out Max, dazzling him

with green light. Max felt his feet leave the ground, and then he was lifted up, up, up towards the monster's gaping mouth.

*This had better work!* Max thought. *Because I've only got one shot!*

He flung the Communicator as hard as

he could. It hit one of the creature's fangs, bounced and hit another, jiggled around inside the silvery metal mouth – and slipped down Tetrax's throat.

*Yes!* Max thought. But Tetrax didn't even notice. It kept pulling Max towards its jaws. The huge, razor-sharp fangs got closer and closer.

*I was too late throwing it*, Max realised. His stomach lurched in horror. The mouth opened wide and Max saw the glistening, crackling teeth rushing towards his face –

From somewhere deep inside of Tetrax there came a muffled boom.

The Robobeast froze. A high-pitched whine split the air. The green ray that held Max wavered and then vanished altogether.

Max plunged downwards, and this time there was no branch to break his fall. He hit the ground with a jolt of pain, then he rolled over and looked up.

Tetrax was standing above him, silent and frozen.

*Done it!*

A great cheer arose from the forest as Naybor and all the other islanders rushed out from among the trees. They gathered round the giant, motionless form of Tetrax, jeering at him and prodding him with their spears.

"Good, Max!" Rivet barked. "Good job!"

In the river, Lia and Spike hugged each other in delight.

Suddenly, Tetrax dropped down onto its six legs, sending the islanders scattering in terror.

Max stayed put. He was wary, but not scared. He guessed what was happening.

Tetrax clawed at the tractor-beam attachment on its head. The attachment fell away and landed on the jungle floor. Then Tetrax spat out the remains of Max's headset. It shook its head and roared.

*It's free*, Max thought. *No longer the Professor's slave.*

The beast slipped into the river and swam away downstream.

Lia watched it go. "He said 'Thank you,'" she told Max.

# CHAPTER NINE

# THE SECRET CITY

Max picked up the Communicator headset. It was coated in Tetrax's thick green spit, and Max had to wipe it clean on a leaf. It was slightly scratched and dented, but he should be able to get it working again. He prised open the casing and reset it.

Naybor and the other islanders crowded round, patting Max on the back, wrapping their long arms around his shoulders and chattering to him.

"They can't stop thanking us!" Lia said. She'd emerged, dripping, from the river. The Verdulans crowded round her too, cooing appreciatively. "They say since we saved them from the monster, they'll do anything we ask now!"

"Ask if they'll give us the key," Max said.

Lia looked at Naybor, wrinkling her

forehead. Naybor smiled, nodded and made a short speech in the Verdulan language.

"He says, of course," Lia translated. "The key didn't save them from the monster – we did. They want us to destroy the key, so that the Kraken's Eye can never be used!"

"One down, three to go," Max said.

"What do you mean?" asked Lia.

"I'll tell you later."

Naybor beckoned to Max and Lia. Then he and the other islanders scampered off into the forest.

"He's taking us to the key," Lia said. "We'll be back soon," she told Spike, who was poking his head out of the river to watch.

"You stay here and keep Spike company," Max said to Rivet. Then he and Lia set off through the forest, trying to catch up with the Verdulans. But the islanders moved with astonishing speed, swinging from branch to branch with their long arms. Max and Lia couldn't possibly keep up. Naybor had to come back every so often to check they were following, and beckon them on.

The trees around them grew thicker and thicker until at last, in the very heart of the forest, they came out into a clearing. Max gasped in amazement.

A strange, beautiful city of yellow stone
stood there in the middle of the jungle. There
were temples with elaborate carvings of birds,
monkeys and strange creatures Max didn't
recognise. There were pyramids, with steps
up the sides. There were statues everywhere,
of the Verdulan people themselves and other
strange forms that Max guessed were their

gods or heroes. The statues were painted, richly decorated with gold jewellery and studded with diamonds and other gems.

"No wonder the pirates and the Professor want to plunder this place!" Max said to Lia. "This stuff must be priceless!"

Lia nodded, gazing about her in wonder.

Naybor led them to a tall statue of a Verdulan king, on a plinth in the courtyard of a temple. His crown was silvery platinum, set with rubies and emeralds. The statue's eyes were sapphires and there was a gleaming yellow topaz on its forehead.

The islanders all gathered around, suddenly silent, as Naybor reached up and pressed the topaz.

There was a whir and a click, and Max grinned as he watched the statue's mouth slowly open.

Naybor reached in and brought out a

massive iron key. The handle and shaft were ornately carved and shaped into fantastic loops and swirls. Naybor dropped the key into Max's outstretched hands. He felt the heavy, serious weight of it. A key of power.

"I'll take it to my father in Aquora," Max said. "He'll know the best way to destroy it."

The islanders bowed to them and waved and smiled. One islander ran forward with a garland of flowers and draped it around Lia's neck. Lia blushed, and Max chuckled.

At last they took their leave of the islanders and went back to the river to pick up Rivet and Spike.

The dogbot barked in greeting and Spike leaped out of the water. Max waded in, found his aquabike and pulled it clear of the reeds.

"Hey!" Lia said. "Look!"

Max's gaze followed her pointing finger. Through a gap in the trees he saw the *Pride of Blackheart* out at sea. It was slowly sailing away, getting smaller and smaller.

"They're going!" said Lia.

"The Professor's control panels must have informed him that we've stopped Tetrax. Without the Robobeast those pirates wouldn't have a hope of conquering the Verdulans," Max said. "They must be moving on to try their luck elsewhere..."

"Try their luck? How?"

"This key's only the first of four," Max explained. "Any one of them will operate the Kraken's Eye. They must be going to look for the next key."

"And where's that?"

"That's just what we don't know," Max said. A thought struck him. "Wait a minute."

He put his Communicator headset on, and twiddled the location-finder. Soon he picked up voices. "I've found them!" Max said. He turned the volume up.

"...So much for your home-made monster!" It was the voice of Cora Blackheart. "Those feeble little swamp-rats were able to beat it!"

"They couldn't have done it alone." That was the Professor's voice. "It was my cursed nephew, he's always throwing a spanner in the works—"

"And who let him escape? You did, you fool!"

"Your pathetic crew weren't much help, were they?" the Professor said angrily.

"Don't argue with me," Cora said, her voice suddenly dangerously quiet. "Your next monster had better do the job for us. Otherwise..."

"He'll learn the true meaning of the word 'pain'!" came the voice of Hook-Hand.

"No," said Cora slowly. "He'll learn the true meaning of the word 'agony'."

There was a short pause. "There'll be no problems next time, I promise," the Professor said, and Max could hear the nervousness in his voice. "My nephew won't be around to interfere. When we get to Arctiria..."

Abruptly, the signal gave out. The ship

must have passed out of range.

Max looked at Lia. "They're going to Arctiria!" he said. "Have you heard of it?"

Lia shook her head. "I don't think so. I don't know the names of the Breather lands. Is it far?"

"It's right up in the north," Max said. "A land of snow and ice. That's where the next key must be. And we have to get there before the pirates!"

"I'd better tell my father where we're going," Lia said.

"If I can re-set the range on this Communicator, I can probably—"

Lia rolled her eyes. "I think we can do better than that." She slid into the river and touched the Pearls of Honour at her chest. Almost immediately, a small black eel popped its head out of the water. *Good thing Lia still has her Pearls*, Max thought. He wondered if he'd ever get his own Pearls back.

Lia looked at the eel for a few moments. Max could tell by the way her forehead creased that she was using her Aqua Powers.

Then the eel sank beneath the river surface again and swam away fast.

"He'll take the message for me," Lia said. "Well – shall we get going? Come on, Spike!"

"Come on, Riv," Max said. "We've got some pirates to deal with!"

He leaped onto the aquabike and revved the engine.

The four of them moved off downriver, towards the open sea.

Max's heart tingled with excitement. Another Sea Quest had begun. He just hoped it wouldn't be his last…

Don't miss Max's next Sea Quest
adventure, when he faces

# NEPHRO
## THE ICE LOBSTER

**FREE COLLECTOR CARDS INSIDE!**

## COLLECT ALL THE BOOKS IN SEA QUEST SERIES 3:

# THE PRIDE OF BLACKHEART

978 1 40832 853 8

978 1 40832 855 2

978 1 40832 857 6

978 1 40832 859 0

# OUT NOW!

Look out for all the books in
Sea Quest Series 4:
# THE LOST LAGOON

### REKKAR THE SCREECHING ORCA
### TRAGG THE ICE BEAR
### HORVOS THE HORROR BIRD
### GUBBIX THE POISON FISH

# OUT IN SEPTEMBER 2014!

Don't miss the
BRAND NEW
Special Bumper Edition:

# SKALDA
## THE SOUL STEALER

978 1 40832 851 4

# OUT IN JUNE 2014

# WIN AN EXCLUSIVE
# GOODY BAG

In every Sea Quest book the Sea Quest logo is hidden in one of the pictures. Find the logos in books 9-12, make a note of which pages they appear on and go online to enter the competition at

## www.seaquestbooks.co.uk

Each month we will put all of the correct entries into a draw and select one winner to receive a special Sea Quest goody bag.

You can also send your entry on a postcard to:

Sea Quest Competition, Orchard Books,
338 Euston Road, London, NW1 3BH

Don't forget to include your name and address!

## GOOD LUCK

Closing Date: May 31st 2014

Competition open to UK and Republic of Ireland residents. No purchase required.
For full terms and conditions please see www.seaquestbooks.co.uk

# DARE YOU DIVE IN?

# www.seaquestbooks.co.uk

Deep in the water lurks a new breed of Beast.

Dive into the new Sea Quest website to play games, download activities and wallpapers and read all about Robobeasts, Max, Lia, the Professor and much, much more.

Sign up to the newsletter at www.seaquestbooks.co.uk to receive exclusive extra content, members-only competitions and the most up-to-date information about Sea Quest.

# IF YOU LIKE SEA QUEST, YOU'LL LOVE BEAST QUEST!

FREE COLLECTOR CARDS INSIDE!

## Series 1: COLLECT THEM ALL!

An evil wizard has enchanted the magical beasts of Avantia. Only a true hero can free the beasts and save the land. Is Tom the hero Avantia has been waiting for?

978 1 84616 483 5

978 1 84616 482 8

978 1 84616 484 2

978 1 84616 486 6

978 1 84616 485 9

978 1 84616 487 3

# DON'T MISS THE
# BRAND NEW SERIES OF:

FREE
COLLECTOR
CARDS
INSIDE!

## Series 14: THE CURSED DRAGON

RAFFKOR
THE STAMPEDING BRUTE

978 1 40832 920 7

VISLAK
THE SLITHERING SERPENT

978 1 40832 921 4

TIKRON
THE JUNGLE MASTER

978 1 40832 922 1

FALRA
THE SNOW PHOENIX

978 1 40832 923 8

# OUT NOW!